Molly Mischief

Saves the World!

GROSSET & DUNLAP
Penguin Young Readers Group
An Imprint of Penguin Random House LLC

Copyright © 2018 by Adam Hargreaves. All rights reserved. First published in the United Kingdom in 2018 by Pavilion Books Limited. First published in the United States in 2019 by Grosset & Dunlap, an imprint of Penguin Random House LLC, 345 Hudson Street, New York, New York 10014. GROSSET & DUNLAP is a trademark of Penguin Random House LLC. Manufactured in China.

Library of Congress Cataloging-in-Publication Data is available.

ISBN 9781524788049   10 9 8 7 6 5 4 3 2 1

Molly Mischief

Saves the World!

Adam Hargreaves

Grosset & Dunlap
An Imprint of Penguin Random House

Hello, my name is **Molly.**
Most of the time I'm happy—happy making mischief.

That's why I'm called **Molly Mischief!**

But some things make me unhappy. Things like chores.

I don't like cleaning my room.
But when I *do* clean my room, Mom's not happy!

There's no pleasing her.

MOLLY!

And I don't like doing the dishes.
But when I *do* the dishes, my brother's not happy.

Sometimes there's no pleasing anyone!

MOLLY!

I wish I could do all my chores in supersonic time.
I wish I had superpowers.
I wish I could be a superhero.

So I went upstairs and got dressed as . . .

SUPER-MOLLY!

I cleaned my bedroom in super-quick time.

I vacuumed.

SUPER-MOLLY!

And dusted.

SUPER-MOLLY!

Put away the dishes,

SUPER-MOLLY!

Mopped, **SUPER-MOLLY!**

And took out the garbage. ALL in the blink of an eye!

I had *lots* of superpowers.

I was very **STRONG.**

I had **LASER EYES.**

I could walk on the ceiling.

Woof! Woof! Woof! Woof! Woof!

I could talk to animals.

I could leap over

TALL

buildings in
a single bound!

And I could fly!

Up! Up! Up!
And away!

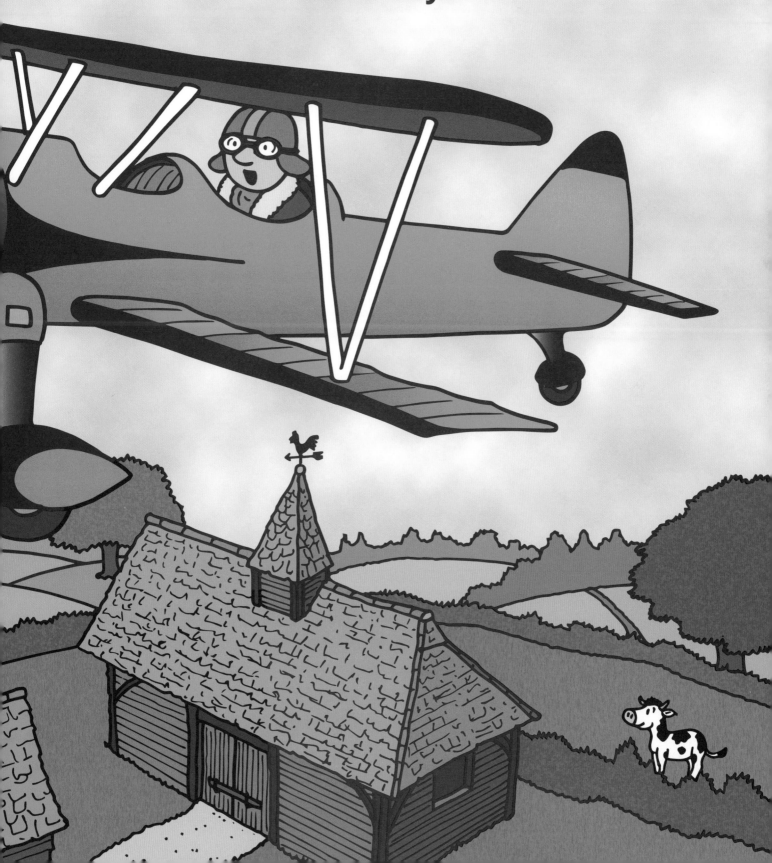

I could fly my kite,
even when there was no wind!

And you should have seen me on my bike!

It was awesome having lots of superpowers.

It was also very useful.
It was useful when the bully at school tried to take my lunch money.

And it was useful when we got stuck in a traffic jam.

I helped old ladies cross the road, at *super speed*.

I saved a cow from a tornado.

MOO!

I rescued a **whale** at the beach!

And I saved the world from
an asteroid!

Super-Molly became super-famous.
She was on the front page of every paper and starred on the TV news.

But nobody knew it was me.
Nobody knew all the good deeds I was doing.
It's no fun being famous and not being recognized.
It's no fun being good and not getting praise.

Being a superhero was also hard work.
I had to get up in the middle of the night to fight crime.

I had to miss my favorite dinner to capture an escaped lion.

And cleaning up a flood was no fun at all.

In fact, being a superhero was just one long list of chores!

So, I gave up being Super-Molly.

I decided it was much easier to do what I'm told.
Well, most of the time.

I *have* kept one superpower.
One superpower I would never give up.
I am super . . .

. . . mischievous!